Cats Are Like That

by Martha Weston

Holiday House / New York

With thanks to Milo, Pickle, Marcel,
Henri, and Tail—inspiration for Fuzzy

and for Deborah—the fairy godmother

Library of Congress Cataloging-in-Publication Data
Weston, Martha.
Cats are like that / Martha Weston.
p.   cm.
Summary: Dot tries to get her new pet fish to do something
interesting while she defends them from the hungry attention of her
cat Fuzzy.
ISBN 0-8234-1419-1 (reinforced)
[1. Cats—Fiction.   2. Fishes—Fiction.   3. Pets—Fiction.]
I. Title.
PZ7.W52645Cat   1999   98-19315   CIP   AC
[E]—dc21

Contents

1 • New Pets

"Look, Fuzzy," said Dot.

"Three fish!

These are my new pets.

They have no hair.

Your hair gets all over.

Cats are like that."

Fuzzy liked his hair all over.

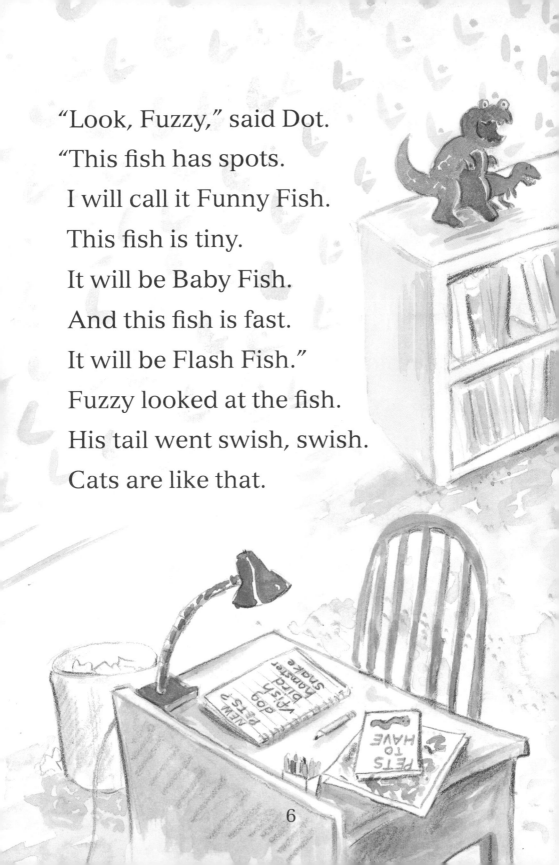

"Look, Fuzzy," said Dot.
"This fish has spots.
I will call it Funny Fish.
This fish is tiny.
It will be Baby Fish.
And this fish is fast.
It will be Flash Fish."
Fuzzy looked at the fish.
His tail went swish, swish.
Cats are like that.

Funny, Baby, and Flash
swam around the bowl.
They went zip, zip,
or they did nothing at all.
"My fish look bored," said Dot.
Fuzzy thought they looked yummy.

"I will get them a book," said Dot.

Fuzzy's tail went swish, swish.

His nose went closer and closer.

Dot came back.

"Bad kitty!" said Dot.

2 • Fish Fun

The fish did not look at the book.

They swam zip, zip,

or they did nothing at all.

"Maybe these fish

want a toy," said Dot.

She saw Fuzzy's ball.

It was a very special ball.

It had a bell inside.

"You can share, Fuzzy," said Dot.
She dropped the ball into the bowl.
The ball stayed on top of the water.
The fish did not play with the ball.
They swam zip, zip,
or they did nothing at all.

"I know!" said Dot.
She put her toy dinosaur
next to the fishbowl.

"They will think
a dinosaur is fun," said Dot.

"Come, Fuzzy, I'll get your supper."
But the supper Fuzzy wanted
was fish.
His tail went swish, swish.

His paw went in the fishbowl.
Dot heard a bell.
She came running back.

The ball with the bell inside
was rolling across the floor.
"Fuzzy!" yelled Dot. "Get down!"

At bedtime Dot said, "I know!
I will build a fence
around the bowl.
Then my fish will be safe."
Dot put more books
near the fishbowl.

She put the dinosaur there, too.

She added a bunny and a truck.

"Now you can't get

into the fishbowl, Fuzzy," said Dot.

Dot rubbed Fuzzy's ears.

"Good night, Fuzzy," she said.

Fuzzy purred.

His tail went swish, swish,

and he went to sleep.

3 • Fish in Danger

In the middle of the night,
Fuzzy woke up.
Cats are like that.
Fuzzy went to see the fish.

His tail went swish, swish.

He jumped up.

The dinosaur fell into the water.

Splash!

The books fell to the floor.

Thump!

The rabbit and the truck fell, too.

Thump! Thump!

Dot woke up.

"Oh, no!" she cried. "What a mess!

Bad kitty! Did you eat the fish?"

Fuzzy sniffed at the toy truck.

Inside the truck was a little fish.

"Baby!" cried Dot.

She put the little fish into the bowl.

He swam zip, zip.
"Baby is okay!" said Dot.
"But where is Funny?
Where is Flash?"

Fuzzy pushed the bunny's ear.

Underneath was a spotted fish.

"Funny is okay!" said Dot.

"But where is Flash?"

Dot crawled around on the floor.

Fuzzy leaped up near the fishbowl.

Flash swam zip, zip
out of the dinosaur's mouth.
"It's Flash!" cried Dot.
"All my fish are okay!
You are a lucky cat, Fuzzy."

4 • The Shelf

The next day Dot said to her mother,
"Fuzzy tried to eat my fish.
He will try again.
Cats are like that."

That afternoon her mother
made a strong shelf.
She hung it high on the wall.
Dot put the fishbowl on the shelf.
"You can't jump on this shelf,"

Dot said to Fuzzy.
"The fish will be safe."
Funny, Baby, and Flash
swam zip, zip.
They swam in and out
of the dinosaur's mouth.

At bedtime Fuzzy found his
ball with the bell inside.
He batted it.
He flipped it.
He rolled it.
He chased it.

Then he sat on it.

Cats are like that.

"Oh, Fuzzy," said Dot.

"Fish can't play with me.

But you can.

Fish can't keep my chin warm.

But you can.

Fish can't even get into trouble.

But you can.

You are a very fine pet."

Fuzzy purred.

Dot rubbed Fuzzy's ears.

Fuzzy snuggled under Dot's chin.

They went to sleep.

Fuzzy liked fish,

but he liked Dot best.

Not all cats are like that.